WHERE BEAR?

by
Sophy Henn

PUFFIN

Once there was a
bear cub....

who lived with
a little boy.

But over time the bear cub grew...

and grew...

AND GREW!

And did things
that bears do...

and do...

AND DO!

One day the boy looked at the bear and realized
he was just too big and bearish to be living
in a house.

"I think it's time we found you a new place to live
where you can be bearish and big,"
said the boy. "But where bear?"

"There are bears in the toy shop,"
said the boy. "The toy shop is great."

"NO"
said the bear.

APPY HARDWARE

92

OPEN

OLS   PLANTS   SEEDS

Lovely Lovely Toy Shop

TOYS
GAMES
MARBLES
BALLS
DOLLS

Open

TOYS
GAMES
MARBLES
BALLS
DOLLS

"Then where bear?" asked the boy.

"Oh, hang on!
There are bears at the zoo!"
said the boy.
"What about the zoo?"

"NO"
said the bear.

"Then where bear?"
asked the boy.

"I've seen bears at the circus,"
said the boy. "What about the circus?"

"I know,
bears live in the woods,"
said the boy.
"What about the
woods bear?"

"NO"
said the bear.

"Then where bear?"
asked the boy.

"Lots of bears live in caves," said the boy. "Would you like to live in a cave?"

"NO"
"NO"
"NO"
"NO"
"NO"
"NO"
"NO" said the bear.

"Then where bear?" asked the boy.

"I think bears
live in the jungle,"
said the boy.
"What do you think bear?"

"NO"
whispered
the bear.

"Then where bear?" asked the boy.

"Hmmm,"
 said the boy.

The bear said nothing.

"I'VE GOT IT!"
said the boy.
"Some bears live in the Arctic.
What about it bear?"

"SNOW"

said the bear.

"There,"
said the boy.

And the boy went home.

So bear was happy.

And the boy was happy.

And they stayed the
very best of friends . . .

. . . chit-chattering
on the phone
all the time.

"We should go somewhere together
like we used to"
said the bear.

"But where bear?"
asked the boy.

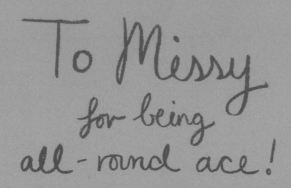

To Missy
for being
all-round ace!

PUFFIN BOOKS
UK | USA | Canada | Ireland | Australia | India | New Zealand | South Africa
Puffin Books is part of the Penguin Random House group of companies
whose addresses can be found at global.penguinrandomhouse.com.
puffinbooks.com
First published 2014
This edition published 2015
001
Text and illustrations copyright © Sophy Henn, 2014
The moral right of the author/illustrator has been asserted
A CIP catalogue record for this book is available from the British Library
Made and printed in Italy
ISBN: 978–0–723–29496–2